# HELP FOR LION

Written by Michèle Dufresne
Illustrated by Max Stasiuk

# Contents

Help for Lion                                2

Help for Lion: The Play                14

Elephants                                   18

Pioneer Valley Educational Press, Inc.

# Help for Lion

One day Giraffe,
Little Monkey, and Elephant
were playing in the jungle.

"Someone is calling
for help," said Elephant.

"Who is it?" said Giraffe.

"It's me, Lion," called Lion.
"I'm down here
in this deep hole."

Giraffe, Little Monkey,
and Elephant looked down
at Lion in the deep hole.

"Please will you help me?"
said Lion. "I can't climb out
of this deep hole."

"We can't help you Lion,"
said Elephant. "You will
eat us after we help you
get out of the hole!"

"No! I will not eat you.
**Please** help me!" said Lion.

5

Giraffe looked down in the hole again. "Hmmm," he said. "The hole is too deep, and we can't get Lion out."

"I have an idea," said Little Monkey. "Elephant, push this big rock into the hole. Lion can get onto the rock and climb out."

Elephant pushed and pushed. The big rock rolled into the hole.

Lion climbed up on top
of the rock.
"I still can't get out,"
he said.

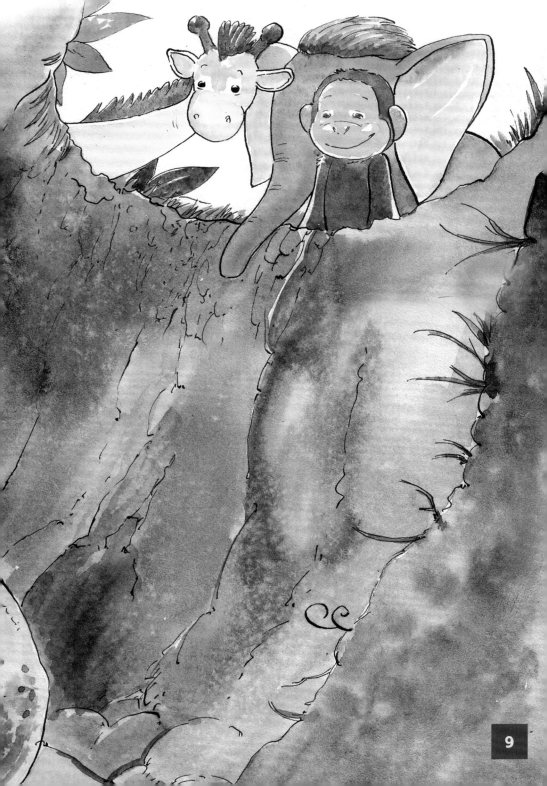

"I have an idea,"
said Giraffe.
"Little Monkey, put your
long tail into the hole."

Little Monkey put his tail
into the hole.

Giraffe held
onto Little Monkey,
and Elephant held onto
Little Monkey, and
Lion held onto
Little Monkey's tail.

They pulled and pulled
and pulled.

Up, up, up came Lion.

"I'm out of the hole,"
said Lion. "Thank you.
But now I am **so** hungry . . ."

# Help for Lion: The Play

One day Giraffe, Little Monkey, and Elephant were playing in the jungle.

Help! Help!

Someone is calling for help.

Who is it?

 It's me, Lion.
I am down here
in this deep hole.

 Look, Lion is down
in a deep hole.

 Please can you help
me? I can't climb
out.

 We can't help Lion.
He will eat us!

 No! I will not eat
you! Please help me.

Hmmm, the hole is deep.

I have an idea. Elephant, you push this big rock into the hole.

Elephant pushed the big rock into the hole.

I still can't get out.

I have an idea. Little Monkey, put your long tail into the hole.

Little Monkey put his tail into the hole. Giraffe and Elephant held onto Little Monkey. Lion held onto Little Monkey's tail. They all pulled and pulled. Up, up, Lion came out of the hole.

Thank you.
But now I am **so** hungry.

# Elephants

Elephants are mammals.
They are big.
They are the biggest
mammals on land.

Elephants can live
a long time.
They can live 70 years.

Elephants can laugh.
Elephants can cry.